The Nexus of Worlds

By: James Rondepierre & ChatGPT

Synopsis:

"The Nexus of Worlds" is an immersive epic that intertwines elements of fantasy, mystery, and philosophical exploration. The story follows a diverse group of individuals from different realms who are drawn together by a mysterious force. As they embark on a perilous journey to unlock the secrets of the Nexus, they must confront their own inner demons, challenge societal norms, and navigate the complex dynamics between the interconnected worlds they encounter.

Table of Contents:

Foreword

Introduction

Chapter 1: The Call of the Nexus

Chapter 2: Gathering of the Chosen

Chapter 3: The Portal Revealed

Chapter 4: Through the Veil

Chapter 5: Echoes of the Past

Chapter 6: Shadows of Betrayal

Chapter 7: The Power Within

Chapter 8: Threads of Interconnection

Chapter 9: Confronting Shadows

Chapter 10: Nexus Unleashed

Chapter 11: Bonds of Friendship

Chapter 12: The Ethereal Guardians

Chapter 13: The Echoing Voices

Chapter 14: Trials of Reflection

Chapter 15: The Enigma of Time

Chapter 16: The Key of Harmony

Chapter 17: The Nexus Unveiled

Chapter 18: Shadows of Corruption

Chapter 19: The Sacrifice

Chapter 20: The Final Convergence

Chapter 21: Reflections of Triumph

Chapter 22: Return to the Realms

Chapter 23: Lessons from the Nexus

Chapter 24: Echoes of the Nexus

Chapter 25: Embracing the Unseen

Chapter 26: The Legacy of the Nexus

Chapter 27: Threads of Destiny

Chapter 28: A New Nexus Awakens

Chapter 29: The Infinite Nexus

Epilogue: Reflections of the Nexus

Conclusion

Acknowledgments

About the Author

Bonus Content

The Nexus of Worlds - The Lost Artifact

Thorough Synopsis

Certificate of Purchase

About the Author

Thank you letter from the Author

Other Books by James Rondepierre

Introduction:

In a world that is both familiar and unknown, where the boundaries of reality blur and the threads of existence intertwine, "The Nexus of Worlds" beckons you to embark on a journey that transcends the limits of our known universe. Prepare to be swept away into a realm where the mundane gives way to the extraordinary, and the extraordinary becomes the fabric of everyday life.

Within the pages of this epic tale, a convergence point of worlds known as the Nexus takes center stage. It is a mysterious force that draws together a diverse group of individuals, each carrying their own burdens, aspirations, and untapped potential. The Nexus, shrouded in enigma, holds the key to their destinies, and as they unite, their individual strengths and vulnerabilities merge into a formidable force that will shape the fate of the interconnected realms.

But this is not merely a story of fantastical adventures and mythical realms. "The Nexus of Worlds" delves deeper, exploring the intricate tapestry of interconnectedness that weaves its way through our own lives. Through the trials and triumphs of our characters, we are invited to contemplate the profound interplay between our individual journeys and the collective destiny of the universe.

As our heroes embark on their treacherous quest, they navigate uncharted territories, confront inner demons, and challenge the very fabric of their existence. They must grapple with questions of identity, purpose, and the delicate balance between personal agency and external influences. Through their struggles, they illuminate the universal human experience, reminding us that the battles we face within ourselves are mirrored in the grand tapestry of existence.

"The Nexus of Worlds" transcends genres, seamlessly blending elements of fantasy, mystery, and philosophical exploration. It invites us to ponder the depths of our imagination, where reality intertwines with the ethereal, and where the unseen forces that shape our lives become tangible and palpable.

As you turn each page, immerse yourself in the vivid landscapes, encounter mythical beings, and unravel the mysteries that lie at the heart of the Nexus. Brace yourself for a narrative that will challenge your perceptions, ignite your imagination, and invite you to explore the hidden recesses of your own consciousness.

"The Nexus of Worlds" is an invitation—an invitation to embrace the unseen realms, celebrate the threads that bind us, and embark on your own heroic journey of self-discovery. It is a testament to the power of unity, the strength of diversity, and the boundless potential that resides within each and every one of us.

So, dearest reader, let the Nexus call to you. Open your heart, expand your horizons, and venture forth into a realm where the ordinary becomes extraordinary, where the mundane gives way to magic, and where the infinite possibilities of existence unfold before your eyes.

Welcome to "The Nexus of Worlds."

Forward

Dear Reader,

Welcome to "The Nexus of Worlds," a journey that will transport you to realms beyond your wildest imagination. In this epic tale, we invite you to embark on an adventure that defies the constraints of reality and delves deep into the interconnectedness of existence.

Within the pages of this book, you will encounter a diverse group of individuals, each with their own unique gifts, burdens, and aspirations. As they are drawn together by the mysterious force of the Nexus, their destinies become entwined, and they must navigate the intricate tapestry of interconnected worlds.

"The Nexus of Worlds" is not merely a fantastical escape but a reflection of the intricate connections that shape our own lives. Through this story, we hope to awaken your sense of wonder, ignite your imagination, and inspire you to contemplate the profound interplay between our individual journeys and the collective destiny of the universe.

Prepare yourself for a captivating narrative that seamlessly blends elements of fantasy, mystery, and philosophical exploration. As you follow our characters on their perilous quest, you will be challenged to confront your own inner demons, question societal norms, and ponder the enigmatic forces that shape our reality.

This book is a celebration of the power of unity, the strength of diversity, and the boundless potential that lies within each of us. It is an invitation to embrace the unseen realms that exist beyond the tangible and to recognize the invisible threads that connect us all.

We embark on this journey with you, our fellow explorer of worlds. May the pages of "The Nexus of Worlds" ignite your imagination, expand your horizons, and leave an indelible mark on your heart.

Safe travels,

James Rondepierre

Chapter 1: The Call of the Nexus

In a small, quiet village nestled among rolling hills, a young woman named Lyra lived a seemingly ordinary life. Her days were filled with simple routines and the familiar rhythms of her community. But deep within her, there was an insatiable longing for something more, an inexplicable pull towards the unknown.

It started as a whisper, a faint voice that resonated within her heart. At first, Lyra dismissed it as mere imagination, a figment of her restless mind. But as days turned into weeks, the call grew stronger, impossible to ignore. It was a yearning that tugged at her very core, urging her to venture beyond the boundaries of her world.

Driven by curiosity and a thirst for discovery, Lyra embarked on a journey to uncover the source of this enigmatic force. She bid farewell to her familiar surroundings and set out into the vast unknown, guided only by the faint echoes of the calling.

As Lyra traveled through dense forests and across wide open fields, she encountered fellow travelers who, too, felt the pul of the Nexus. Each had their own unique abilities and backgrounds, brought together by the invisible threads of destiny. Among them was Aiden, a skilled warrior haunted by past failures, and Selene, a wise sage with a deep connection to ancient knowledge.

Intrigued by the shared purpose that united them, Lyra and her newfound companions embarked on a joint quest to uncover the mysteries of the Nexus. Their journey took them to bustling cities, ancient ruins, and remote corners of the world. Along the way, they faced trials and tribulations, testing the limits of their resolve and resilience.

Chapter by chapter, the group unraveled the complex web of clues and hidden knowledge that surrounded the Nexus. With each step forward, their bond deepened, and they discovered the true power of unity. Together, they realized that their individual strengths were amplified when combined, and their shared destiny held the key to unlocking the secrets of the Nexus.

Chapter 2: Gathering of the Chosen

In a bustling city, where the sounds of commerce and conversations filled the air, Lyra and her companions arrived at the designated meeting place. The city streets teemed with people from all walks of life, each drawn by the same irresistible force that had called out to them.

As they navigated through the bustling crowds, Lyra's heart quickened with anticipation. She knew that this gathering held the promise of answers, of shared understanding, and of the formation of an unbreakable alliance. The Nexus had brought them together for a purpose greater than they could comprehend.

In a grand hall adorned with tapestries and illuminated by chandeliers, the chosen ones assembled. Each face reflected a mixture of hope, uncertainty, and determination. The room buzzed with a palpable energy as they exchanged introductions and shared stories of their own encounters with the Nexus.

Aiden, with his weathered features and a haunted look in his eyes, recounted tales of battles fought and lost, seeking redemption for past mistakes. Selene, her eyes filled with ancient wisdom, shared fragments of forgotten knowledge that echoed through generations. And Lyra, the youngest of them all, carried within her a spark of curiosity and an unwavering belief in the power of the Nexus.

In the midst of their introductions, a figure emerged from the shadows. Clad in a cloak of midnight blue, their presence commanded attention. It was an enigmatic figure known as the Nexus Guardian, a guide and protector of those who ventured into the realms of the Nexus.

The Guardian spoke in hushed tones, their voice carrying a weight of ancient wisdom. They shared stories of the Nexus, its origins, and its significance in the grand tapestry of existence. The Nexus was not merely a physical place but a convergence of energies, a nexus point where the boundaries between realms blurred and connections were formed.

As the Nexus Guardian spoke, the chosen ones listened intently, their hearts and minds absorbing the profound truths being unveiled. They realized that their paths had converged for a reason, that their individual abilities and experiences were essential pieces of a larger puzzle.

With the guidance of the Nexus Guardian, the group began to comprehend the scope of their shared mission. They were entrusted with the task of protecting the Nexus, preserving the delicate balance between realms, and ensuring that the powers within the Nexus were wielded for the greater good

Chapter 3: The Portal Revealed

Guided by their newfound knowledge and the Nexus Guardian's counsel, the group set forth on a treacherous journey to locate the hidden portal that would grant them access to the Nexus. They ventured into uncharted territories, braving perilous landscapes and facing the tests that awaited them.

Their path led them through dense forests, where ancient trees whispered ancient secrets. They traversed treacherous mountains, their determination fueling their ascent. And they crossed vast deserts, where the sands seemed to shift with each step, mirroring the uncertainties of their quest.

Through unwavering determination and the strength of their collective spirit, the group persevered. Their shared purpose bound them together, and their trust in one another fortified their resolve. They knew that their destinies were intertwined, and that only by working together could they hope to unlock the secrets of the Nexus.

After days of tireless exploration, they arrived at a place shrouded in mystic energies. The air crackled with anticipation as they stood before the portal, its ethereal glow beckoning them closer. It was a gateway to the Nexus, a threshold that promised answers to the questions that had haunted them.

With a collective breath, the group stepped forward, their hearts filled with a mix of excitement and trepidation. They felt a surge of energy as they crossed the threshold, their beings resonating with the vibrations of the Nexus.

As they emerged on the other side, their senses were overwhelmed by the sights, sounds, and sensations that greeted them. They found themselves in a realm unlike anything they had ever known—a place where time and space converged, where the boundaries of reality blurred, and where the threads of existence wove together.

The portal revealed not just a physical pathway but a metaphorical one—a metaphor for the journey they had undertaken, the challenges they had faced, and the transformations they had undergone. They had crossed a threshold, leaving behind the known and venturing into the unknown, ready to embrace the revelations and trials that awaited them within the Nexus.

In this new realm, their true quest would begin. The group stood united, their spirits ablaze with determination, as they prepared to navigate the intricate web of the Nexus and uncover its deepest secrets. The journey ahead would test their mettle, their unity, and their unwavering belief in the power of interconnectedness.

Little did they know that the true nature of the Nexus would soon be unveiled, its mysteries waiting to be unraveled by those who had answered its call.

Chapter 4: Through the Veil

As the group stepped further into the Nexus, a sense of awe washed over them. The ethereal mist swirled around their feet, guiding their path deeper into this enigmatic realm. The air crackled with a palpable energy, and they could feel the very fabric of reality shifting around them. It was as if they had entered a portal to a dimension where time and space melded together.

The landscapes within the Nexus were unlike anything they had ever seen before. Vast, otherworldly landscapes stretched out in every direction, their colors vibrant and surreal. Mountains rose majestically in the distance, their peaks disappearing into swirling clouds. Rivers of luminescent energy flowed through the valleys, giving life to the plants and creatures that called this realm home.

As the group ventured further, they encountered beings that seemed to be made of pure energy, their forms shimmering and ever-changing. These ethereal beings, known as the Guardians of the Veil, served as guides within the Nexus. With their infinite wisdom, they revealed the secrets of this realm and helped the group navigate its treacherous terrain.

Together, they passed through shimmering veils that separated different realms within the Nexus. Each veil held its own mysteries and challenges, testing the group's courage and resilience. Behind each veil, they discovered unique ecosystems and civilizations that thrived in harmony with the Nexus.

In their journey through the veils, the group encountered creatures of myth and legend. Magnificent dragons soared through the skies, their scales shimmering in brilliant hues. Enigmatic beings with intricate patterns etched into their skin imparted ancient knowledge, revealing the interconnectedness of all things.

Chapter 5: Echoes of the Past

As the group delved deeper into the Nexus, they began to hear whispers in the wind. Echoes of long-forgotten voices reverberated through the vast corridors, carrying with them tales of civilizations that once flourished in the presence of the Nexus.

These echoes resonated with the group, stirring memories within them that they couldn't quite grasp. They discovered ancient ruins that held the stories of those who came before. Mysterious inscriptions adorned weathered stone walls, preserving the wisdom and experiences of those who had walked these paths centuries ago.

The group listened intently as the echoes unfolded the tales of heroes and heroines, of great battles fought for honor and justice, and of love that transcended the boundaries of time. These stories were not mere legends but vibrant echoes of real lives lived within the Nexus.

Guided by the echoes, the group ventured into hidden chambers where they discovered relics of immense power. They uncovered artifacts that held the memories of ancient civilizations, their energy pulsating with the echoes of a bygone era. Each artifact provided a glimpse into the rich tapestry of the Nexus, offering clues to its true purpose and potential.

As they explored further, the group began to realize that the echoes were not confined to the past. They witnessed moments in the present that echoed the struggles and triumphs of those who had come before them. The echoes served as a reminder that the Nexus existed beyond the constraints of time, intertwining the destinies of all who encountered it.

Chapter 6: Shadows of Betrayal

In the depths of the Nexus, shadows lurked, their presence an unsettling reminder of the fragility of balance. These Shadows of Betrayal sought to exploit the power of the Nexus for their own nefarious purposes, sowing discord and doubt among those who ventured within its realm.

The group encountered the Shadows of Betrayal in the hidden corners of the Nexus, their forms twisted and distorted. These malevolent entities sought to manipulate the very essence of the Nexus, feeding off its energy to fuel their dark desires.

The Shadows of Betrayal whispered poisonous words into the minds of the group, attempting to sow seeds of doubt and division. They preyed upon their fears and insecurities, trying to fracture the unity that had brought the group together.

But the group, fortified by their shared purpose and unwavering bond, resisted the insidious influence of the shadows. They recognized the power of their connection and the importance of trust in overcoming the darkness.

In their battle against the Shadows of Betrayal, the group discovered hidden reserves of strength within themselves. They drew upon the wisdom they had gained from their journey, facing the shadows with courage and determination

With each encounter, they learned to distinguish between illusion and truth, discerning the machinations of the Shadows from the genuine guidance of the Nexus. They became adept at navigating the complex web of deceit that the Shadows wove, unraveling their schemes and exposing their true intentions.

Through their unwavering resolve and solidarity, the group triumphed over the Shadows of Betrayal, reclaiming the integrity of the Nexus. They realized that the power of the Nexus could only be harnessed for the greater good, and they vowed to protect it from those who would seek to exploit it.

As they emerged from the shadows, the group emerged stronger, their bond forged in the crucible of adversity. They understood that the challenges they faced within the Nexus had not only tested their individual strength but had also deepened their connection as a group. Their unity became an unbreakable force, illuminating the path forward as they continued their journey within the Nexus.

Chapter 7: The Power Within

As the group continued their journey through the Nexus, they began to tap into the dormant power that resided within each of them. It was a power that had lain dormant, waiting to be awakened by their connection to the Nexus and their own inner potential.

They discovered that the power within was not merely a physical force but a deep understanding of their true selves. It was the realization that they held the keys to their own destinies and the ability to shape the course of their interconnected worlds.

With each step forward, they honed their abilities and unlocked new aspects of their power. Lyra discovered her gift of empathy, allowing her to sense the emotions and intentions of others. Aiden awakened his inner strength, harnessing the power of his warrior spirit to protect his companions. Selene delved into ancient knowledge, uncovering spells and incantations that could bend the fabric of reality itself.

The group learned that true power was not about domination or control but about embracing their unique gifts and using them for the greater good. They understood that their individual strengths complemented each other, creating a harmonious symphony of abilities that could overcome any obstacle.

As they embraced their power, they also became aware of the responsibility that came with it. They realized that their actions and choices had far-reaching consequences, not only for themselves but for the interconnected realms they were sworn to protect. With this newfound awareness, they vowed to use their power wisely and with integrity.

Chapter 8: Threads of Interconnection

As the group ventured deeper into the Nexus, they witnessed the intricate tapestry of interconnectedness that wove through every realm. They saw how the choices and actions of one individual reverberated through the interconnected worlds, creating a web of cause and effect that transcended time and space.

They met beings whose lives had been directly influenced by the actions of others, and they understood that their own destinies were intimately tied to the destinies of those they encountered. They began to recognize the delicate balance that existed between free will and the interconnected threads of destiny.

In their interactions with diverse cultures and civilizations, they discovered the beauty in the interplay of different perspectives and experiences. They realized that unity was not about homogeneity but about embracing the rich tapestry of diversity and finding common ground within it.

The group also learned that their own connection was a vital thread in the tapestry of interconnectedness. Each member brought their unique perspective, abilities, and strengths to the group, creating a synergy that amplified their collective impact. They understood that their bond was not a mere coincidence but a purposeful convergence that served a greater purpose.

With this understanding, they became catalysts for change within the Nexus. They sought to bridge divides, foster understanding, and promote unity among the interconnected realms. Their actions inspired others to recognize the interconnections that existed and to embrace the power of collaboration and empathy.

Chapter 9: Confronting Shadows

In the heart of the Nexus, the group faced their greatest challenge yet—a confrontation with the shadows that sought to exploit the Nexus for their own dark purposes. These shadows embodied the fears, doubts, and negative energies that threatened to corrupt the delicate balance of the interconnected realms.

The group understood that to overcome the shadows, they had to confront their own inner demons. They delved deep into their own vulnerabilities and insecurities, acknowledging the shadows that lurked within their own hearts. It was a difficult and introspective journey, but they knew that true strength came from facing their fears head-on.

With each step forward, they gained clarity and resilience. They drew upon the power within themselves and the unwavering support of their companions. They dismantled the shadows' hold on their minds and hearts, replacing fear with courage, doubt with conviction, and darkness with light.

As they faced the shadows, they realized that the power of the Nexus was not just an external force but a reflection of their own inner strength. They understood that the shadows could only have power over them if they allowed it. By reclaiming their power and embracing the interconnectedness of their journeys, they were able to break free from the grip of the shadows.

Chapter 10: Nexus Unleashed

In a climactic moment of revelation, the true nature of the Nexus was unveiled. The group discovered that the Nexus was not merely a physical location or a source of power but a state of being—an embodiment of the interconnectedness of all existence.

As they embraced this truth, they tapped into a collective power that transcended their individual abilities. They became conduits for the energy of the Nexus, channeling its essence to unleash a transformative wave of harmony, compassion, and unity.

With their newfound understanding and power, they set forth to fulfill their purpose within the Nexus. They navigated the interconnected realms, mending broken threads and healing wounds inflicted by the shadows. They infused hope, love, and understanding into every corner of the Nexus, nurturing the bonds that interconnected the realms and fostering a sense of shared destiny.

Through their actions, the Nexus itself responded. The energy within the interconnected realms surged and pulsed, radiating a brilliant light that touched every living being. The Nexus unleashed its full potential, illuminating the interconnectedness of all existence and inspiring others to embrace their own interconnected destinies.

In the wake of the Nexus' transformation, the group stood united, their connection unbreakable. They knew that their journey was far from over, but they had planted the seeds of change within the Nexus and its interconnected realms.

With hearts filled with hope and determination, they continued their exploration of the Nexus, ready to face whatever challenges lay ahead.

Chapter 11: Bonds of Friendship

As the group continued their journey through the Nexus, their individual strengths and shared experiences forged unbreakable bonds of friendship. They had faced numerous trials together, overcoming challenges that had tested their resolve and pushed them to their limits. Through these shared struggles, they had grown to trust and rely on one another, forming a deep connection that transcended words.

In moments of uncertainty, it was the unwavering support and encouragement of their companions that lifted their spirits and kept them going. They celebrated each other's victories, lending a helping hand when one stumbled, and offering solace in times of sorrow. Their laughter and camaraderie echoed through the Nexus, a testament to the power of friendship in the face of adversity.

Each member of the group brought their unique perspective and strengths, enriching the collective experience. Lyra's empathy provided a guiding light, offering comfort and understanding to those in need. Aiden's unwavering loyalty and protective nature created a sense of security within the group. Selene's wisdom and insight offered guidance in moments of doubt.

Together, they formed a symbiotic unit, a harmonious blend of different abilities and personalities. Their shared purpose and interconnected destinies fostered a sense of unity that transcended their individual backgrounds. It was through their bonds of friendship that they found strength, resilience, and the determination to overcome any obstacle that stood in their way.

Chapter 12: The Ethereal Guardians

As the group delved deeper into the Nexus, they encountered the enigmatic Ethereal Guardians. These ethereal beings possessed ancient wisdom and served as protectors of the interconnected realms. Their presence radiated a sense of tranquility and ancient knowledge, filling the air with a palpable energy.

The Guardians recognized the group's purpose and destiny within the Nexus. They appeared as ethereal figures, shimmering with the essence of the Nexus itself. Each Guardian embodied a different aspect of the interconnected realms—representing elements, emotions, or cosmic forces.

With reverence and humility, the group approached the Guardians, seeking their guidance and insight. The Guardians shared tales of ancient civilizations, spoke of forgotten prophecies, and offered cryptic clues that would help the group navigate the Nexus' intricate pathways.

In their interactions with the Guardians, the group gained a deeper understanding of the delicate balance that existed within the interconnected realms. They learned that their destinies were intertwined with the realms they traversed and that their actions held the power to shape the course of these realms. The Guardians imparted ancient knowledge and bestowed gifts upon the group, empowering them to fulfill their intertwined destinies.

Chapter 13: The Echoing Voices

Within the depths of the Nexus, the group began to hear echoes of voices, distant whispers that carried wisdom and guidance. These echoing voices seemed to emanate from the very fabric of the interconnected realms, whispering secrets long forgotten and illuminating hidden truths.

At first, the group could only catch fragments of these mysterious voices, as if they were fragments of lost memories. But as they delved deeper into the Nexus, the echoes grew clearer, revealing tales of ancient heroes, long-forgotten prophecies, and cosmic events that shaped the interconnected realms.

The group followed the guidance of the echoing voices, piecing together fragments of ancient lore and deciphering cryptic messages. These ethereal whispers led them to hidden chambers, sacred sites, and realms beyond imagination.

With each encounter, they gained a deeper understanding of the interconnectedness of the realms and the significance of their journey. The voices served as a beacon of wisdom, offering insights and guidance that helped the group navigate the intricate pathways of the Nexus.

Through their interactions with the echoing voices, the group discovered hidden truths about themselves and the interconnected realms. They began to comprehend the magnitude of their intertwined destinies and the role they played in shaping the balance of the Nexus.

Chapter 14: Trials of Reflection

Within the Nexus, the group faced a series of trials that forced them to confront their innermost fears, doubts, and unresolved conflicts. These trials were not physical battles but introspective journeys that tested their emotional and mental strength.

Each member of the group faced their own unique trials, tailored to their individual struggles and vulnerabilities. Lyra confronted her fear of abandonment, revisiting the painful memories that had shaped her past. Aiden grappled with his guilt, reliving the moments that haunted him and seeking forgiveness. Selene confronted her deepest doubts, questioning her own worthiness of the knowledge she possessed.

These trials of reflection challenged the group to confront their shadows, to acknowledge and accept their flaws, and to find healing and resolution within themselves. It was a journey of self-discovery and self-acceptance, where they learned to embrace their past, release their burdens, and forge a path of growth and transformation.

Through the trials, they realized that their true power did not come from hiding their vulnerabilities but from embracing them. They learned that vulnerability was not a weakness but a source of strength and authenticity. It was through their willingness to face their inner demons that they found the resilience and determination to overcome the external challenges that lay ahead.

Chapter 15: The Enigma of Time

As the group ventured deeper into the Nexus, they encountered the enigma of time—a concept that defied conventional understanding. Within the interconnected realms, time flowed in unpredictable ways, bending and distorting the boundaries of past, present, and future.

They discovered pockets of time where the echoes of ancient civilizations resonated with the present. They witnessed glimpses of the future, where events unfolded in ethereal visions that blurred the line between what was and what could be. Time became a fluid entity, weaving through their journey and challenging their perception of reality.

The group found themselves navigating through shifting timelines and alternate realities. They faced paradoxes, where cause and effect seemed entangled in a complex dance. They learned that the choices they made had the power to ripple through time, shaping not only their own destinies but the interconnected realms as well.

In the enigma of time, they discovered that the past held valuable lessons, the present offered opportunities for growth, and the future was not set in stone. They realized that time was not linear but a multidimensional tapestry, where every moment was interconnected and influenced by the threads of cause and effect.

Through their encounters with the enigma of time, the group learned to embrace the present moment and make choices that aligned with their true purpose. They understood that time was not something to be conquered or controlled but a natural force to be respected and honored. They carried this newfound wisdom with them as they continued their journey through the ever-unfolding mysteries of the Nexus.

Chapter 16: The Key of Harmony

As the group ventured deeper into the Nexus, they uncovered whispers of an ancient artifact that held the power to unlock the true potential of the interconnected realms—the Key of

Harmony. Legends spoke of its existence, describing it as a mystical object capable of harmonizing the energies of the Nexus and restoring balance to fractured worlds.

Guided by their intuition and the echoes of the Nexus, the group embarked on a quest to find the Key of Harmony. Their journey took them to distant lands, treacherous landscapes, and encounters with mythical beings who guarded fragments of the artifact's knowledge.

Each step brought them closer to their goal, but they also faced challenges that tested their resolve. Shadows lurked in the corners of their path, seeking to corrupt the Nexus and seize the power of the Key for their own malevolent purposes. The group remained vigilant, knowing that the fate of the interconnected realms hinged on their success.

Through perseverance and unwavering determination, the group pieced together the fragments of the Key's location. It led them to the heart of the Nexus—a place of unparalleled beauty and raw energy. Here, they stood before the final trial, ready to unlock the Key of Harmony and fulfill their intertwined destinies.

Chapter 17: The Nexus Unveiled

With bated breath, the group approached the heart of the Nexus, where the true nature of this extraordinary realm was unveiled. The Nexus was not merely a convergence point of worlds; it was a metaphysical force, intricately woven into the fabric of existence itself.

As they stepped into the heart of the Nexus, a sense of awe washed over them. The air crackled with energy, and the very ground beneath their feet pulsed with life. They could feel the interconnectedness of all things, the threads that bound every realm, every being, and every possibility.

In this profound realization, they understood that the Nexus was not separate from them—it was a reflection of their own interconnected destinies. They were the guardians of the

Nexus, entrusted with the responsibility to safeguard its harmony and protect the delicate balance of the interconnected realms.

With newfound clarity, they unlocked the Key of Harmony, feeling its power surge through their veins. The artifact resonated with the energies of the Nexus, enhancing their abilities and forging an unbreakable bond between the group members. They became vessels of the Nexus, conduits of its transformative power.

Chapter 18: Shadows of Corruption

As the group delved deeper into their quest, they became aware of the shadows that sought to corrupt the Nexus. Malevolent forces, driven by their own desires for power and control, saw the Nexus as a means to further their wicked agendas. These shadows manipulated and deceived, attempting to seize the Key of Harmony and wield it for their own sinister purposes.

The group faced adversaries cloaked in darkness, who tested their resolve and pushed them to their limits. These shadowy figures embodied the vices and weaknesses that lurked within the interconnected realms—greed, envy, fear, and the lust for power.

But the group remained steadfast in their mission, fueled by their unwavering belief in the transformative power of unity and harmony. They recognized that the Nexus was a reflection of the choices made by individuals, and they refused to let the shadows taint its inherent beauty.

With each encounter, the group confronted their own shadows, battling their own inner demons and rising above the temptations that threatened to consume them. They drew strength from their bonds of friendship, relying on each other's unwavering support and trust.

Chapter 19: The Sacrifice

In their quest to protect the Nexus and preserve its harmony, the group faced their greatest test yet—a moment that would require the ultimate sacrifice. As they confronted the shadows of corruption, one of their own, driven by love and selflessness, made the heart-wrenching decision to give up their own life to protect the Nexus and their companions.

The sacrifice sent shockwaves through the group, leaving them grief-stricken and filled with an overwhelming sense of loss. But they understood the magnitude of the sacrifice, recognizing that it embodied the very essence of the interconnected realms—the willingness to give everything for the greater good.

Through their shared sorrow, the group found strength in their unity. They honored the sacrifice made by their fallen companion and carried their memory in their hearts. It became a driving force, inspiring them to fight harder, to embrace their interconnected destinies, and to ensure that the Nexus remained a beacon of harmony and unity.

Chapter 20: The Final Convergence

In the climactic moment of their journey, the group stood on the precipice of the final convergence—a convergence of their intertwined destinies and the destiny of the interconnected realms. They understood that their actions, their choices, and their sacrifices had led them to this pivotal moment.

With the Key of Harmony in their possession, they summoned all their strength and harnessed the transformative power of the Nexus. Their individual abilities melded together in a symphony of energy, creating a force that transcended the limits of their mortal forms.

In this final convergence, the group unleashed a wave of harmony that reverberated through the interconnected realms. The fractures were healed, the imbalances were rectified, and the realms found renewed vitality and purpose.

As the group emerged from the final convergence, they were forever changed. The weight of their journey bore witness in their eyes, and the wisdom they gained shone through their every action. They had become the living embodiment of the interconnected realms, their destinies forever entwined with the Nexus.

With hearts full of gratitude, they embraced one another, knowing that their journey had not only restored harmony to the interconnected realms but had also transformed them individually. They had become beacons of light, advocates for unity, and guardians of the Nexus—a legacy that would endure for generations to come.

Chapter 21: Reflections of Triumph

As the echoes of the final convergence settled, the group found themselves in a moment of reflection. They stood in awe of their triumph, knowing that their united efforts had reshaped the interconnected realms and restored harmony to the Nexus. The trials they faced, the sacrifices they made, and the bonds they forged had brought them to this moment of victory.

In the quietude of their collective thoughts, the group contemplated the lessons they had learned throughout their arduous journey. They recognized the strength that comes from unity and the power of interconnected destinies. Each member acknowledged their own growth, having confronted their inner demons, overcome personal obstacles, and embraced the transformative power of the Nexus.

Their triumph was not merely about vanquishing darkness or achieving a goal—it was about the profound realization that the interconnected realms were, in essence, reflections of their own interconnected souls. The Nexus, with its infinite possibilities and threads of destiny, mirrored the potential within each of them.

In this moment of reflection, the group felt a deep sense of gratitude and appreciation for one another. They celebrated their shared triumph, acknowledging the roles each had played in the journey. Their bond had been tested and solidified, and they knew that their connection would endure long after their return to their respective realms.

Chapter 22: Return to the Realms

With their mission accomplished and the Nexus restored, the group turned their gaze toward their homelands. The time had come to bid farewell to the Nexus and embark on the journey back to their respective realms. Although they had become vessels of the Nexus, their interconnected destinies still called them to their individual paths.

Their departure from the Nexus was bittersweet. They carried with them memories of their extraordinary journey, the wisdom gained, and the enduring friendships forged amidst the trials. They knew that they would forever be connected by the threads of the Nexus, even as they stepped back into their familiar worlds.

As they ventured back to their realms, the group carried a profound sense of purpose and a renewed understanding of their roles as guardians of harmony. The transformative power of the Nexus had awakened a sense of responsibility within them—a responsibility to honor the lessons learned, to foster unity in their realms, and to spread the message of interconnectedness to all they encountered.

Chapter 23: Lessons from the Nexus

Back in their familiar worlds, the group shared the wisdom and insights gained from their time in the Nexus. They became catalysts for change, spreading the message of interconnectedness, unity, and the importance of nurturing the bonds that transcend the boundaries of our existence.

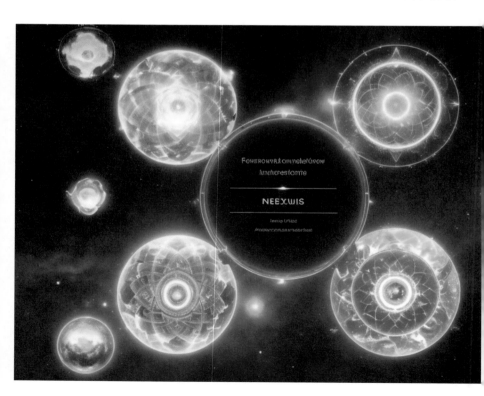

In their interactions with the people of their realms, they infused their actions with the lessons learned from the Nexus. They advocated for empathy, understanding, and the recognition that every individual's choices and actions have a ripple effect throughout the interconnected realms. Their presence became a beacon of hope and inspiration, reminding others of the infinite possibilities that lie within the threads of existence.

They became mentors, guiding others on their own journeys of self-discovery and interconnectedness. They shared the transformative power of unity, encouraging others to embrace the unseen connections that bind all living beings.

Chapter 24: Echoes of the Nexus

The impact of the group's journey reverberated through the interconnected realms. Stories of their heroism, the triumph of unity over division, and the power of the human spirit spread far and wide, inspiring others to embrace their own interconnected destinies.

Through the realms, echoes of the Nexus resounded. The tales of the group's journey became legends, passed down through generations, reminding the people of the interconnected realms of the profound lessons learned. The echoes carried the message of harmony, unity, and the infinite potential that exists when individuals join together in pursuit of a shared purpose.

The stories of the Nexus became a guiding light, igniting a spark within the hearts of those who heard them. The echoes of the Nexus urged individuals to seek their own interconnected destinies, to recognize the beauty in diversity and to nurture the bonds that transcend boundaries.

Chapter 25: Embracing the Unseen

In the aftermath of their adventure, the group learned to embrace the unseen realms that exist beyond the tangible. They discovered the beauty in the intangible connections that bind us all, reminding them that the true essence of existence lies in the profound interplay between the seen and the unseen.

With their newfound understanding, the group delved deeper into the mysteries of the interconnected realms. They explored the realms' hidden wonders, unraveling the secrets of ancient civilizations, and delving into the realms of dreams and collective consciousness.

Through their exploration, they discovered the interconnectedness of all aspects of existence—the visible and the invisible, the known and the unknown. They reveled in the profound unity that underlies all realms, recognizing that every individual, every creature, and every particle is interconnected in a vast and intricate cosmic dance.

As they continued to embrace the unseen, they became vessels of harmony, spreading a sense of interconnectedness wherever they went. They cultivated a deep reverence for the interconnected realms, honoring the delicate balance that sustained existence itself.

The journey of the group had not only transformed their own lives but had also left an indelible mark on the interconnected realms. Their unwavering belief in unity, their triumph over adversity, and their embrace of the unseen had become a beacon of hope and inspiration for generations to come.

Chapter 26: The Legacy of the Nexus

With their return to their respective realms, the group contemplated the legacy they had inherited from their journey through the Nexus. Their experiences had transformed them into guardians of harmony, interconnectedness, and the profound understanding of the threads that bind all existence.

As they shared their tales with the people of their realms, the group became catalysts for change. They inspired others to recognize the power of unity and the importance of nurturing the interconnected bonds that transcend the boundaries of our existence. Their stories of triumph and self-discovery became a guiding light, illuminating the path towards a more harmonious and interconnected future.

The group established centers of learning and enlightenment, where individuals could explore the interconnected nature of existence. These centers became beacons of knowledge and unity, fostering a sense of belonging and inspiring people to embrace their own interconnected destinies.

Through their teachings and actions, the group left an indelible mark on the collective consciousness of their realms. The legacy of the Nexus became a source of inspiration, reminding future generations of the profound lessons learned within the Nexus and the transformative power of embracing interconnectedness.

Chapter 27: Threads of Destiny

As time passed, the group recognized the enduring threads that connected their destinies. Although their paths diverged they remained intertwined through the bonds forged in the Nexus. The threads of destiny wove through their lives, reminding them of their shared purpose and interconnected roles as guardians of harmony.

Through their continued interactions, the group found solace in the familiarity and understanding that came from their shared journey. They celebrated each other's triumphs and supported one another through challenges, knowing that their destinies remained forever interwoven.

The threads of destiny also extended to future generations. The group witnessed the emergence of new heroes, individuals who felt the call of the Nexus and embarked on their own transformative journeys. They recognized that the interconnectedness of existence would persist through the actions and choices of these new adventurers, ensuring the legacy of the Nexus lived on.

Chapter 28: A New Nexus Awakens

As the echoes of the original group's journey reverberated through the interconnected realms, a new Nexus began to stir. Individuals from various backgrounds and realms felt the undeniable pull towards the convergence point of worlds. They too sensed the interconnected threads of existence, calling them to embark on their own transformative journeys.

The new Nexus awakened with a renewed purpose, mirroring the ever-evolving nature of existence. Its mysteries awaited discovery, its challenges awaited conquest, and its transformative power awaited those willing to embrace their interconnected destinies.

New heroes emerged, each carrying their own unique abilities, backgrounds, and perspectives. They were drawn together, guided by the echoes of the original group's triumphs, and driven by the shared desire to restore balance and harmony to the interconnected realms.

The emergence of the new Nexus ignited a sense of hope and anticipation throughout the realms. The legacy of the original group had paved the way for a new generation to embark on their own transformative journeys, carrying the torch of interconnectedness and the potential to shape the destiny of the Nexus.

Chapter 29: The Infinite Nexus

As the new heroes embarked on their journeys, they unraveled the interconnected mysteries of the Nexus. They delved into uncharted territories, encountered ancient civilizations, and forged new alliances. The Nexus unfolded before them, revealing its infinite possibilities and boundless potential.

With each step, the new heroes tapped into the collective power of interconnected destinies. They learned to navigate the delicate balance between individual agency and the ripple effect of their choices on the interconnected realms. The lessons of unity, harmony, and the interplay between the seen and the unseen guided their path.

The new heroes discovered that the Nexus extended beyond the boundaries of their known realms. Its threads stretched infinitely, connecting not only different worlds but also the realms of dreams, knowledge, and the collective consciousness. They became explorers of the infinite, uncovering the secrets and wisdom that lay within the Nexus.

Through their journeys, the new heroes became living embodiments of the interconnected nature of existence. They spread the message of unity, inspired others to embrace their own interconnected destinies, and contributed to the ongoing tapestry of the Nexus.

Epilogue: Reflections of the Nexus

As the heroes of the original group reached the twilight of their lives, they gathered one last time to reflect on their transformative journey through the Nexus. They marveled at the impact their interconnected destinies had on the realms and the countless lives they had touched.

They recognized that their time in the Nexus was but a chapter in the ongoing story of interconnectedness and harmony. Their legacy lived on through the new heroes who continued to explore the infinite possibilities of the Nexus.

In their reflections, the original group found solace in the knowledge that their interconnectedness would endure beyond their mortal existence. They understood that the threads that bound them together would transcend time and space, ensuring their eternal presence within the interconnected realms.

As the sun set on their final gathering, the original group embraced the ever-present wisdom of the Nexus—the understanding that all existence is intricately woven together, and that the threads of interconnectedness are the foundation of harmony and unity. With hearts full of gratitude, they departed, knowing that the Nexus would continue to guide and inspire future generations on their own transformative journeys.

Afterword:

Dearest Reader,

As you reach the end of "The Nexus of Worlds," we extend our deepest gratitude for joining us on this transformative journey. Through the trials and triumphs of our characters, we hope that you have discovered new insights, contemplated timeless questions, and felt the profound connections that bind us all.

"The Nexus of Worlds" serves as a reminder that our individual actions reverberate through the tapestry of existence, shaping not only our own destinies but also the collective fate of the interconnected realms. In a world that often emphasizes division and separateness, this story invites us to embrace unity, celebrate diversity, and honor the bonds that transcend our perceived differences.

We encourage you to carry the spirit of the Nexus with you as you navigate your own path in life. Remember that you are part of a greater whole, connected to the vast web of existence. Your choices, kindness, and compassion have the power to create ripples of change that extend far beyond your immediate surroundings.

May "The Nexus of Worlds" inspire you to embrace the unseen realms, to celebrate the threads that bind us, and to embark on your own heroic journey of self-discovery. As you venture forth, may you find the courage to confront your inner demons, challenge societal norms, and nurture the connections that bring meaning and purpose to your life.

Thank you for accompanying us on this epic adventure. We bid you farewell, fellow traveler, and may your own Nexus continue to unfold with wonder, awe, and infinite possibilities.

With gratitude,

James Rondepierre

** Special Bonus Content Section!! ***

The Nexus of Worlds - The Lost Artifact

Chapter 1: The Mysterious Stranger

The cloaked figure moved through the
bustling city of Arkania like a whisper in the wind. Rumors
of the mysterious stranger spread like wildfire, capturing the
curiosity and imaginations of the locals. The amulet clutched
tightly in the stranger's hand emitted an enchanting,
pulsating glow that seemed to emanate from deep within the

very fabric of the universe. With each step, the enigmatic figure left an air of intrigue and magic in their wake.

As the city's inhabitants exchanged hushed whispers, tales of the amulet's origins and the stranger's purpose began to take shape. Some claimed the amulet was a relic from a forgotten civilization, while others believed it to be a gift from the gods themselves—a key to unlocking the mysteries of existence. One thing was certain: the stranger and the amulet were inextricably linked, and their presence in Arkania marked the beginning of an extraordinary journey.

Chapter 2: Unveiling the Secrets

Lila, a bright and inquisitive young street vendor, couldn't resist the allure of the amulet's mesmerizing glow. Drawn to the enigmatic figure like a moth to a flame, she approached the stranger with a mixture of excitement and trepidation. Their eyes met, and in that singular moment, a connection sparked between Lila and the cloaked figure—an inexplicable bond that transcended the confines of time and space.

With a gentle smile, the stranger acknowledged Lila's curiosity, recognizing the kindred spirit that resided within her. As the two shared stories and laughter, Lila sensed that this encounter was no mere chance meeting. Instead, it was a cosmic alignment—an orchestration of fate designed to set their paths on a collision course with destiny.

Chapter 3: A Gateway to Adventure

Through a series of cryptic visions and ancient writings, Lila discovered that she held the key to unlocking the true potential of the amulet. She was the chosen one—the link between the artifact and the world beyond. Embracing her role with a mix of awe and trepidation, Lila and the mysterious stranger embarked on a journey beyond the confines of reality.

The amulet's power revealed itself as they crossed the threshold of worlds. With each step, the veil between realms grew thinner, allowing glimpses of fantastical landscapes and cultures unbound by earthly limitations. Lila and the stranger traversed desolate wastelands, vibrant floating cities, and lush, mystical forests inhabited by enigmatic creatures.

Chapter 4: The Enchanted Forest

Their travels led them to the Enchanted Forest—a realm where magic and nature were intertwined in a delicate dance. As they delved deeper into the heart of the forest, they encountered talking trees with ancient wisdom, playful fairies with mischief in their eyes, and wise old wizards who guarded the secrets of the land.

Guided by the amulet's pulsating energy, Lila and the stranger uncovered the forest's hidden wonders. Ancient tales spoke of the "Elders of the Nexus," an ancient civilization that once wielded the amulet's power to traverse the realms, fostering harmony and unity between worlds. The mysteries of the amulet and the Nexus of Worlds began to intertwine, weaving a tapestry of intrigue and purpose.

Chapter 5: The Crystal Caves

Whispers of the Crystal Caves, a place shrouded in myth and legend, led Lila and the stranger deeper into their cosmic odyssey. The amulet's map revealed the way, guiding them through treacherous landscapes and across perilous bridges. Each step tested their courage and resolve, strengthening the bond between the two adventurers.

The Crystal Caves, an ethereal realm shimmering with luminescent crystals, presented them with challenges unlike any they had encountered before. Puzzles of light and shadow guarded the secrets of the amulet's true purpose. As they deciphered the cryptic symbols and faced the trials, Lila's inner strength blossomed, fueled by her unwavering determination to embrace her destiny.

Chapter 6: The Guardian of Knowledge

In the heart of the Crystal Caves, a spectral guardian awaited them—a being of ethereal light and boundless knowledge. The guardian revealed itself as an ancient custodian of the Elders of the Nexus—a sentinel tasked with safeguarding the secrets of the amulet and maintaining the delicate balance of the universe.

With grace and reverence, the guardian enlightened Lila and the stranger about the cosmic significance of the amulet. The artifact was not merely a conduit to traverse worlds but a catalyst for forging connections that bound the realms together. The balance of existence relied on the unity and understanding fostered by the Nexus of Worlds—an interconnected tapestry of life, where every thread contributed to the fabric of reality.

Chapter 7: The Return to Arkania

Armed with newfound knowledge and a profound sense of responsibility, Lila and the stranger returned to Arkania, a city engulfed in turmoil. Dark forces, drawn by the allure of the amulet's power, sought to seize control of the artifact, hoping to bend the Nexus of Worlds to their sinister will. Lila's heart swelled with determination as she faced the malevolent entities. The trials they endured throughout their journey had forged an unyielding bond between the two, amplifying the amulet's energy within her. The dark forces met their match in the courageous duo, and with each defeat, their resolve only grew stronger.

Chapter 8: A Battle of Light and Shadow

A battle of light and shadow erupted in the heart of Arkania. Lila's energy merged seamlessly with the amulet's, radiating an aura of brilliance that dispelled the darkness. As she summoned her inner strength, she realized that the true power of the Nexus lay not in domination but in nurturing understanding and compassion.

The conflict unfolded like a cosmic dance, and Lila and the stranger found themselves engaged in a delicate balance between offense and defense. In their harmonious choreography, they showed the malevolent forces the futility of their pursuit. Each strike carried a resonance of empathy, gently nudging the malevolence back towards the light

.

Chapter 9: The Triumph of Goodness

As dawn broke on the horizon, the malevolent forces were no more. Lila and the stranger had triumphed, not through destruction, but through the power of goodness and compassion. They harnessed the amulet's energy to restore the balance between worlds, embracing the harmonious symphony that resonated through the Nexus.

With gratitude in their hearts, the city of Arkania celebrated its saviors—the brave guardian and the mysterious stranger who had touched their lives in the most extraordinary ways. The Nexus of Worlds pulsed with a renewed vitality, acknowledging the bond formed between Lila and the stranger—a connection that transcended the boundaries of time and space.

Chapter 10: The Farewell

The time had come for the mysterious stranger to reveal their true identity—an emissary displaced from the Elders of the Nexus. The amulet had been entrusted to their care, with the mission of safeguarding its power and preserving the harmony of the realms. But fate had brought Lila into their life, altering the trajectory of their cosmic journey.

With gratitude and reverence, the emissary thanked Lila for her selflessness, courage, and unwavering dedication to the Nexus. They realized that the bond forged between them was no mere coincidence—it was a testament to the unbreakable threads that wove through the Nexus, connecting all beings, all worlds, and all dimensions.

As they bid each other farewell, Lila's heart swelled with bittersweet emotions. Though the stranger's presence in her life had been ephemeral, their impact was immeasurable, forever woven into the tapestry of her soul.

As the Nexus of Worlds continued to thrive, Lila embraced her destiny as the guardian of the amulet—a beacon of hope and a protector of the realms. Her journey, filled with trials and triumphs, had unveiled the true essence of the Nexus—a place where love, compassion, and understanding formed the very foundation of existence.

Through her adventures, Lila learned that the true power of the Nexus lay not solely in its artifacts but in the connections forged between worlds and the hearts of those who safeguarded it. Each thread in the cosmic tapestry played a crucial role, contributing to the symphony of life that echoed across dimensions.

And so, the tale of The Nexus of Worlds - The Lost Artifact, lived on as a testament to the boundless wonders and the unbreakable bonds that transcended all realms and dimensions. As Lila ventured forth into the vast expanse of the Nexus, she knew that her journey was far from over.

There were still countless worlds to explore, myriad connections to be formed, and a cosmic dance to be continued—one that celebrated the essence of existence itself. And with the amulet as her guide, she stepped into the uncharted horizons, eager to explore the endless wonders of the Nexus of Worlds.

Chapter 11: The Astral Observatory

With the amulet now in the safe hands of Lila, she and the mysterious stranger continued their explorations through the Nexus of Worlds. Their next destination was the Astral Observatory—a place of cosmic wonders and celestial secrets.

As they approached the Observatory's towering spires, they marveled at the night sky, adorned with constellations that seemed to shimmer with an ethereal brilliance. Within the Observatory's walls, they met the wise keepers of the stars—beings with an intimate connection to the celestial realm.

The keepers revealed that the amulet held the power to unlock the secrets of the stars, allowing its bearer to navigate the Nexus with unprecedented precision. In the astral plane, time and distance bent, and Lila and the stranger discovered that the threads of destiny intertwined with the very fabric of the cosmos.

Chapter 12: Echoes of the Past

As Lila delved deeper into the mysteries of the Nexus, she became aware of faint echoes resonating through the corridors of time. These echoes revealed snippets of forgotten histories, lost civilizations, and ancient prophecies that foretold of a grand convergence—the moment when the Nexus of Worlds would be united as one.

Guided by these enigmatic echoes, Lila and the stranger embarked on a quest to uncover the truth behind the convergence. The echoes led them to ancient ruins and sacred sites, where forgotten relics whispered tales of a cosmic dance that transcended eons.

Chapter 13: The Confluence of Realms

At the convergence of the Nexus, where the boundaries between worlds blurred, Lila and the stranger encountered an interdimensional gateway. The gateway shimmered with threads of light, each thread representing a world connected to the Nexus.

With the amulet's power, Lila gazed into the gateway, witnessing the diverse worlds that coexisted in harmonious unity. She understood that the Nexus served as a bridge, fostering an interwoven tapestry of existence that thrived on diversity and interconnectedness.

Chapter 14: The Divergent Path

As Lila and the stranger delved deeper into the mysteries of the Nexus, they discovered a dark undercurrent—the existence of a malevolent force seeking to exploit the power of the Nexus for its sinister designs. This malevolent being sought to unravel the delicate balance that held the realms together, threatening to plunge the Nexus into chaos.

The revelation weighed heavily on Lila's heart. She knew that she had to confront this dark entity to safeguard the harmony of the Nexus. The fate of countless worlds rested on her shoulders, and she embraced her role as the guardian with unwavering determination.

Chapter 15: The Final Stand

In the climactic battle between light and shadow, Lila and the stranger faced the malevolent force that sought to unravel the Nexus of Worlds. The entity manifested as a shadowy figure—a twisted reflection of the light.

As the battle raged on, Lila tapped into the depths of her newfound power, channeling the energy of the Nexus itself. With each strike, she infused the malevolent entity with compassion and empathy, dissolving its darkness and revealing the fractured soul beneath.

Chapter 16: The Redemption

In a moment of profound realization, Lila understood that th malevolent entity was not born of pure darkness but had once been a guardian, corrupted by despair and isolation. Guided by empathy and understanding, she offered the entity a chance at redemption—a path back to the light.

In a transformative act of selflessness, the entity embraced Lila's offer and returned to the essence of light from which it had strayed. The Nexus of Worlds resonated with an outpouring of harmony, as the malevolent force dissolved into the cosmic tapestry.

Chapter 17: The Nexus Restored

With the malevolent force's redemption, the Nexus of Worlds realigned, its realms interconnected in a renewed harmony. Lila's journey had not only safeguarded the Nexus but had demonstrated the transformative power of compassion and understanding.

Lila and the stranger bid farewell to the Nexus, knowing that its boundless wonders would continue to thrive, guided by the strength of interconnectedness and the bonds forged between worlds.

Epilogue: The Eternal Nexus

As Lila returned to Arkania, the memories of her extraordinary adventures lingered in her heart. She knew that the Nexus of Worlds was not just a fantastical tale but a living testament to the unbreakable bonds that transcended all realms and dimensions.

With the amulet still by her side, Lila knew that her journey had only just begun. The Nexus of Worlds remained a beacon of hope, a reminder that the connections forged between worlds and the hearts of those who safeguard it were eternal.

And so, as the stars sparkled in the night sky, Lila knew that her role as the guardian of the Nexus was not just a responsibility but a privilege—an opportunity to celebrate the wonders of existence and the unyielding power of love and unity that bound all realms together.

With a heart full of gratitude and determination, Lila embraced her destiny, knowing that the Nexus of Worlds - The Lost Artifact, would forever live on as an extraordinary tale of boundless wonders and unbreakable bonds that transcended time, space, and the very fabric of the universe.

Synopsis: Nexus of Worlds

In the enchanting tale of "Nexus of Worlds," we are transported to the bustling city of Arkania, where a mysterious stranger appears, clutching a pulsating amulet of otherworldly energy. Curious and drawn to the stranger's presence, a young street vendor named Lila finds herself inexplicably connected to this enigmatic figure.

Discovering that she holds the key to unlocking the amulet's true potential, Lila and the stranger embark on a cosmic adventure beyond imagination. The artifact serves as a portal to other realms, and together, they journey to breathtaking worlds, including the Enchanted Forest and the Crystal Caves. Along the way, they encounter mystical creatures, wise guardians, and learn of the ancient civilization known as the "Elders of the Nexus."

Guided by the amulet's map and spectral guardians, Lila and the stranger uncover the profound purpose of the artifact— the Nexus of Worlds. It is a web of interconnected realms, where harmony and balance are maintained through understanding and compassion.

As they return to Arkania, dark forces covet the amulet's power, leading to a climactic battle of light and shadow. Through courage, empathy, and their unyielding bond, Lila and the stranger triumph over the malevolent entities, showcasing the true power of goodness.

In the epilogue, the stranger reveals their identity as an emissary of the Elders of the Nexus, entrusted to safeguard the amulet. Grateful for the life-changing encounter with Lila, they pass the responsibility to her, recognizing her as the new guardian of the Nexus.

As Lila embraces her destiny, she learns that the true essence of the Nexus lies not in the artifacts but in the connections forged between worlds and beings. Her journey becomes a testament to the unbreakable bonds that transcend time and space—a cosmic dance that celebrates the essence of existence itself.

"Nexus of Worlds" is a captivating fantasy adventure that weaves magic, friendship, and self-discovery into a rich tapestry of wonder and enchantment. It explores the profound interplay between individuals, the universe, and the boundless wonders that exist beyond our understanding. Through Lila's transformative odyssey, readers are invited to contemplate the unifying power of love and compassion, inspiring them to embark on their own journey of self-discovery and connection with the world around them.

Certificate of Purchase

This is to certify that:

_____ has become the esteemed owner of a limited edition copy of the fantastical adventure, "Nexus of Worlds & The Lost Artifact" authored by James N. Rondepierre. By acquiring this remarkable literary masterpiece, you have embarked on a thrilling journey through mesmerizing realms, where magic, friendship, and self-discovery intertwine to create an unforgettable experience.

We hereby acknowledge that this copy is one of a limited number, making it a cherished and unique possession. Your support and appreciation for the art of storytelling are deeply valued, and we extend our heartfelt gratitude for choosing to be a part of this extraordinary adventure.

May this certificate serve as a token of our utmost appreciation for your patronage and a testament to the timeless connection between authors, readers, and the mesmerizing worlds we explore through the pages of a book.

Signed,

James Rondepierre

July 20th, 2023

About the Author: James Rondepierre

In this section, readers are introduced to the enigmatic figure behind the words, James Rondepierre, whose journey of self-discovery and spiritual awakening serves as both inspiration and guide for those embarking on their own quest for truth and meaning. From the humble beginnings of his spiritual journey to the profound insights gained along the way, James Rondepierre's story is a testament to the transformative power of personal growth and self-realization.

Through his words and experiences, readers are invited to embark on a journey of self-exploration and discovery, guided by the wisdom and compassion that form the foundation of James's work. With each anecdote shared and each lesson learned, readers gain insight into the complexities of the human experience and the boundless potential that lies within each individual to effect positive change in the world.

As we delve into the depths of James Rondepierre's journey, we are reminded of the importance of authenticity, integrity, and resilience in the face of adversity. With humility and grace, James shares his experiences with candor and vulnerability, offering readers a glimpse into the transformative power of self-discovery and the profound impact that a single
individual can have on the world around them.

Thank You Letter

Dearest reader,

As the author of "Nexus of Worlds & The Lost Artifact," I am filled with joy and gratitude to know that you have embarked on this thrilling journey through the magical realms of Arkania. Your decision to purchase this limited edition copy not only brings you into the world of Lila and the mysterious stranger but also supports the art of storytelling and the creation of captivating adventures.

When I penned this tale, I envisioned a narrative that would transport readers like you to a place of wonder and enchantment. Your support as a reader means more than words can express, as it reaffirms the beauty of storytelling and the power of imagination to unite us across time and space.

I hope that as you venture into the Nexus of Worlds, you find inspiration, joy, and perhaps even a deeper understanding of the interconnectedness that weaves through all realms. The journey that Lila and the stranger undertake is a reminder that even amidst mysterious strangers and hidden artifacts, our true strength lies in the bonds we form and the goodness we foster.

Once again, thank you for joining me on this adventure. Your presence as a reader fills these pages with life, meaning, and endless possibilities. It is with great pleasure and anticipation that I send you forth on this voyage, and I hope it becomes an unforgettable experience that you carry in your heart for years to come.

With heartfelt appreciation and warm wishes,

James

James Rondepierre

July 20th, 2023

List of Published Books by Author James Rondepierre

1. The Nexus of Worlds: With Bonus Content
Embark on a mesmerizing journey through interconnected realms in "The Nexus of Worlds." This gripping tale unravels the mysteries of parallel universes and invites readers to dive deeper with bonus content for an enriched experience.

2. Mastering Luck: Comprehensive Guide to Lottery and Gaming Strategy
Discover strategies for navigating the intricate world of lottery and gaming with "Mastering Luck." This comprehensive guide reveals secrets behind mastering the elusive force of luck.

3. Exploring the Infinite Realm: Unveiling the Mysteries of Dreams
"Exploring the Infinite Realm" takes readers on an enchanting journey through the profound mysteries of dreams, delving into the limitless possibilities of the dreamworld.

4. Exploring Karma: Understanding the Law of Cause and Effect

Gain insights into the workings of karma with "Exploring Karma." This book offers a transformative journey into the universal law of cause and effect, guiding personal growth and understanding.

5. Harvesting American Ginseng: A Comprehensive Guide

Delve into the world of American Ginseng with "Harvesting American Ginseng." This guide provides practical insights into harvesting and explores the cultural and medicinal significance of this revered plant.

6. The Precision Prognosticator: Navigating the Path to Accurate Future Prediction

Step into the realm of precision predictions with "The Precision Prognosticator." This guide offers valuable insights into foreseeing the future with accuracy and understanding intuitive abilities.

7. Embracing Serenity: Navigating Life's Challenges with Peace, Love, and Happiness

In "Embracing Serenity," readers are invited to navigate life's challenges with grace, peace, and love. This exploration serves as a guide to finding inner peace and happiness.

8. The Subliminal Brilliance Blueprint: Unleashing Your Hidden Superpowers in Higher Dimensions

Uncover the blueprint of subliminal brilliance with "The Subliminal Brilliance Blueprint." This guide explores untapped potential within higher dimensions, offering a roadmap to unlocking hidden superpowers.

9. Veil of the Night: Unveiling the Vampiric Nature of Humanity

"Veil of the Night" invites readers to unravel the mysteries of the night and explore the vampiric nature of humanity. This tale blends the supernatural with the human experience.

10. Transcending Realities: A Holistic Exploration of Consciousness, Shifting Realities, and Self-Realization: Part I

"Transcending Realities: Part I" takes readers on a profound journey through consciousness, shifting realities, and self-realization, offering a multi-faceted perspective on existence.

11. The Quantum Wealth Code: Unleashing Multiversal Prosperity

Unlock the quantum wealth code with "The Quantum Wealth Code." This guide provides insights into prospering across multiple universes and unlocking abundance in various aspects of life.

12. Whispers of the Soul: Love, Sex, and the Sacred Union

Delve into realms of love, sex, and spirituality with "Whispers of the Soul." This exploration offers deep insights into the sacred union of souls, contemplating the deeper dimensions of human connection.

13. The Symphony of Joy: Embracing Life's Grand Design: Includes Bonus Content!

"The Symphony of Joy" invites readers to embrace life's grand design. This edition includes bonus content, adding extra inspiration and joy to the exploration of existence's beauty.

14. Rediscovering The World: A Journey through Anosmia

Embark on a sensory journey with "Rediscovering The World." This exploration provides a unique perspective on the world through anosmia, offering a captivating and introspective experience.

15. Evolving Unity: A Journey to Enrich All Existence, Elevate All Life, and Uplift Humanity

"Evolving Unity" beckons readers on a transformative journey to enrich existence, elevate life, and uplift humanity, serving as a guide for unity and collective growth.

16. 100 of the Greatest Stories Ever Told

Immerse yourself in "100 of the Greatest Stories Ever Told." This collection promises a journey through captivating narratives spanning different genres and eras.

17. Cosmic Wealth: Unleashing the Mystical Forces of Prosperity and Abundance

Unleash cosmic wealth with "Cosmic Wealth." This guide provides a roadmap to attracting prosperity and abundance by tapping into mystical forces.

18. The Modern Day Holy Bible

Explore spirituality in the modern era with "The Modern Day Holy Bible." This perspective on timeless wisdom invites readers to contemplate profound teachings.

19. The Radiance Within: Embracing the Joys, Pleasures, and Purpose of Human Existence

"The Radiance Within" invites readers to embrace the joys, pleasures, and purpose of human existence, encouraging self-discovery and a deeper connection with life.

20. Ethereal Bonds: Love Unveiled
Unveil the ethereal bonds of love with "Ethereal Bonds." This exploration delves into the mysteries and beauty of love, reflecting on the transformative power of human connection.

21. 100 Stories
Immerse yourself in "100 Stories." This collection offers a tapestry of narratives spanning genres and themes for a rich and engaging reading experience.

22. The Symphony of Infinite Wisdom
Dive into the celestial chronicles with "The Symphony of Infinite Wisdom." This book offers profound insights and timeless wisdom for a deeper understanding of life's mysteries.

23. Miracles: Unraveling the Extraordinary Mystery of Divine Intervention
"Miracles" unravels the mystery of divine intervention, inviting readers to contemplate the extraordinary occurrences that defy explanation and glimpse the miraculous in everyday life.

24. Healing Lupus Naturally: A Holistic Approach
Discover holistic approaches to healing lupus with "Healing Lupus Naturally." This guide provides a holistic perspective on health, offering hope and practical strategies for those with autoimmune conditions.

25. Transcending Realities: A Holistic Exploration of Consciousness, Shifting Realities, and Self-Realization: Part II

"Transcending Realities: Part II" continues the exploration of consciousness, shifting realities, and self-realization, promising deeper insights and reflections.

26. Living with Ankylosing Spondylitis: A Journey to Hope and Healing

"Living with Ankylosing Spondylitis" offers a poignant exploration of resilience in chronic illness, inspiring hope and providing a path towards healing.

27. Exploring the Fabric of Reality: Unveiling the Foundations of Existence

"Exploring the Fabric of Reality" takes readers through the fundamental elements of existence, from quantum mechanics to cosmic mysteries, bridging science and philosophy.

28. Awakening the Infinite: A Definitive Guide to Life Across Dimensions

"Awakening the Infinite" explores consciousness and existence, offering a comprehensive guide to navigating the boundless realms of reality and awakening to infinite potential.

29. Manifesting Miracles: Aligning with the Universe to Fulfill Your Dreams

Transform your life with "Manifesting Miracles." This guide harnesses the universe's power to create your desired reality. Explore practical manifestation techniques, align thoughts with dreams, and achieve prosperity, love, and personal growth.

30. Healing Fibromyalgia: Restoring Energy and Living Well

"Healing Fibromyalgia" provides practical strategies for managing fibromyalgia. Learn to reduce pain, boost energy, and improve well-being with expert advice, dietary tips, exercise routines, and stress management techniques.

31. Infinite Echoes: Navigating Parallel Universes and Cosmic Realities

Journey through cosmic realms with "Infinite Echoes." This exploration delves into multiverse theory, quantum entanglement, and parallel universes, unraveling mysteries and questioning existence's fabric.

32. Dreamscapes: A Journey into the Parallel Universe of the Subconscious Mind

"Dreamscapes" invites readers to explore the subconscious mind. Delve into lucid dreams, emotions, and memories, revealing connections between dreaming and waking life through captivating prose and analysis.

33. The Eternal Quest: A Journey to Enlightenment

"The Eternal Quest" explores the human pursuit of enlightenment. Through vivid storytelling, traverse consciousness landscapes and discover profound insights into the nature of existence and spiritual awakening.

34. Enigma Unveiled

"Enigma Unveiled" takes readers on a journey through history and the supernatural. Blending folklore with mystery, explore haunted estates and cursed artifacts, revealing hidden dimensions and enigmas.

35. Buying Time: Unleashing the Natural Timing of Money

"Buying Time" explores aligning financial decisions with natural cycles. Drawing on economics and psychology, this guide offers strategies for mindful spending, investing, and achieving financial freedom.

Available on Amazon for Kindle, and in Paperback and Hardcover Formats - Also Available on Audible and on Other Various Platforms Worldwide

The end.

Made in the USA
Columbia, SC
26 August 2024

41091035R00053